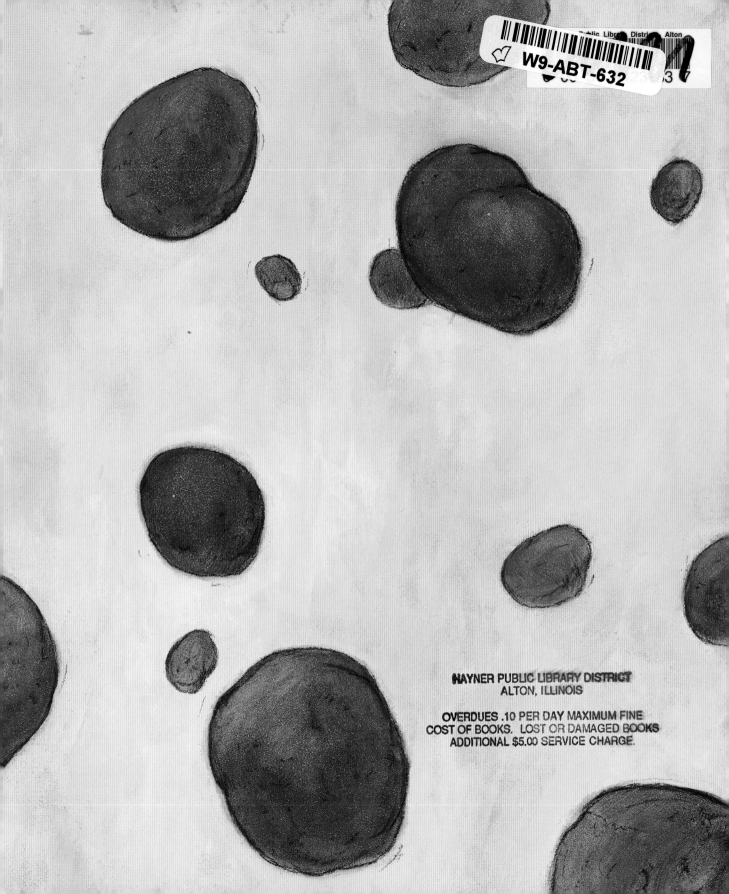

Pigs
Love
Potatoes

Anika Denise *illustrated by* Christopher Denise

Philomel Books

For our own little piggies—
Sofia and Isabel—who bring life and laughter
to our kitchen, everyday.
—Mom and Dad

ONE pig wants potatoes
So Mamma starts to cook.

Then one pig's little brother
Decides to come and look.

Now TWO pigs want potatoes
And soon begin to yelp
So Mamma scolds her two pigs
And tells them they must help.

Two pigs wash potatoes
While Mamma gets a pan
When two pigs' little sister
Sings "Catch me if you can!"

Now THREE pigs peel potatoes
And Mamma gets a spoon

To stir the three potatoes
That will be boiling soon.

Just then the Pappa Piggy
Comes through the big brown door.
He sits down at the table
Making three pigs into FOUR.

Now four pigs peel potatoes

And four pigs sit and wait

When four pigs' next-door neighbor
Comes strolling through the gate.

Now FIVE pigs want potatoes
Plus Mamma makes it SIX.

That's quite a few potatoes
That Mamma has to fix.

Then three *more* little piggies
Show up just in time
And Mamma adds potatoes
SEVEN, EIGHT and NINE.

"Nine potatoes for nine piggies,"
Says Mamma with a grin.
Add one more for good measure
S p l a s h !
In goes number TEN!

Well, since pigs love potatoes
To Mamma's great delight

The very piggy piggies
Eat each and every bite.

The only thing that Mamma tells
Her piggies they must do

Is kiss her cheek and clear their plates
When piggies are all through.

Patricia Lee Gauch, editor

PHILOMEL BOOKS

A division of Penguin Young Readers Group.   Published by The Penguin Group.
Penguin Group (USA) Inc., 375 Hudson Street, New York, NY 10014, U.S.A.
Penguin Group (Canada), 90 Eglinton Avenue East, Suite 700, Toronto, Ontario, Canada M4P 2Y3 (a division of Pearson Penguin Canada Inc.).
Penguin Books Ltd, 80 Strand, London WC2R 0RL, England.
Penguin Ireland, 25 St. Stephen's Green, Dublin 2, Ireland (a division of Penguin Books Ltd.).
Penguin Group (Australia), 250 Camberwell Road, Camberwell, Victoria 3124, Australia (a division of Pearson Australia Group Pty Ltd).
Penguin Books India Pvt Ltd, 11 Community Centre, Panchsheel Park, New Delhi - 110 017, India.
Penguin Group (NZ), Cnr Airborne and Rosedale Roads, Albany, Auckland 1310, New Zealand (a division of Pearson New Zealand Ltd).
Penguin Books (South Africa) (Pty) Ltd, 24 Sturdee Avenue, Rosebank, Johannesburg 2196, South Africa.
Penguin Books Ltd, Registered Offices: 80 Strand, London WC2R 0RL, England.

Text copyright © 2007 by Anika Denise.   Illustration copyright © 2007 by Christopher Denise.

Design by Semadar Megged.   The art was created with acrylic and charcoal on board.   The text is set in 23-point Goudy Old Style.
Library of Congress Cataloging-in-Publication Data

ISBN 978-0-399-24036-2
1 3 5 7 9 10 8 6 4 2
First Impression